From a Distance

JULIE GOLD

illustrated by JANE RAY

With an appreciation by Nanci Griffith

Dutton Children's Books ⌒ New York

For children of all ages all around the world
            —JULIE GOLD

and for
Connect Humanitarian Agency
working in Bosnia
            —JANE RAY

Text copyright © 1998 by Julie Gold
Appreciation copyright © 1998 by Nanci Griffith
Illustration copyright © 1998 by Jane Ray
All rights reserved.

The words of the song "From a Distance" copyright © 1987 by Julie Gold are reproduced by kind
permission of the publishers, Wing & Wheel Music and Cherry River Music o/b/o Julie Gold Music, BMI.

Special thanks to Peter W. Primont, George Edward Regis, Burt Stein, and Alan Koenig.
Love and thanks to Clara and Ellen Temple for additional artwork.

CIP Data is available.

Published in the United States 1999 by Dutton Children's Books,
a division of Penguin Putnam Books for Young Readers,
345 Hudson Street, New York, New York 10014
Conceived, designed, and produced by The Albion Press Ltd, England
Originally published in the UK 1998 by Orchard Books, London
Color origination by Culver Graphics, High Wycombe, England
Printed in Hong Kong/China by South China Printing Co. (1988) Ltd.
First American Edition
ISBN 0-525-45872-7   10 9 8 7 6 5 4 3 2 1

Connect Humanitarian Agency has supplied new and donated books
to all the major libraries and schools throughout Bosnia Herzegovina.
Further information on Connect can be obtained from
20 St. Leonard's Bank, Edinburgh EH8 9SQ, Scotland, UK.

I truly believe that when you love what you do, you do it with God. I love music. I love writing songs.

I grew up in the sixties and I have vivid memories of all that was happening in the world then: the Vietnam War, the Civil Rights Movement, the Women's Movement, the Space Program, the Beatles. When I recall those memories, I recall the songs that were popular at the time, and it's as if those songs actually orchestrated those events. All my memories come with a soundtrack.

I wrote "From a Distance" in 1985. It was the culmination and outpouring of all my vivid memories and experiences. I am honored to receive all the loving responses it has elicited over the years, and I hope I am managing that love in a responsible way. It thrills me to think that a little song I wrote in a one-room apartment right before my thirtieth birthday has brought so much joy to children of all ages all around the world.

Maybe someday we will all live in a world that has no guns, no bombs, and no diseases— that's my hope of hopes.

—JULIE GOLD

F ROM A distance
The world looks blue and green
And the snow-capped mountains white

From a distance
The ocean meets the stream
And the eagle takes to flight

From a distance, there is harmony
And it echoes through the land

It's the voice of hope
It's the voice of peace
It's the voice of every man

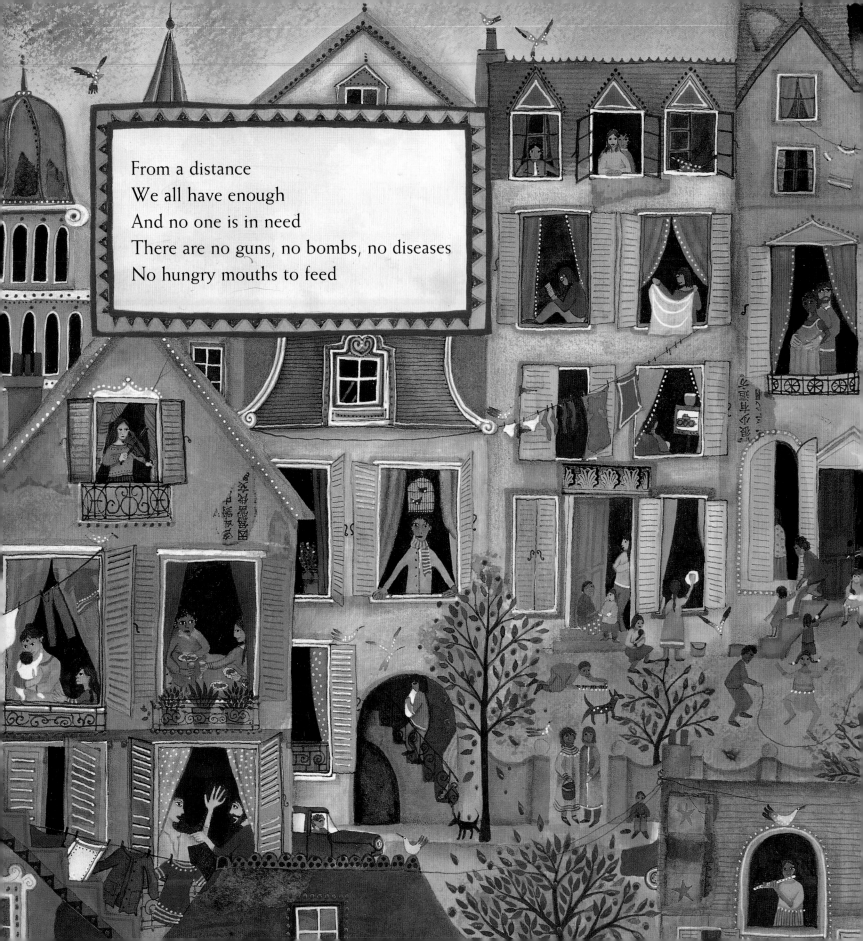

From a distance
We all have enough
And no one is in need
There are no guns, no bombs, no diseases
No hungry mouths to feed

From a distance, we are instruments
Marching in a common band
Playing songs of hope
Playing songs of peace
They're the songs of every man

God is watching us, God is watching us
God is watching us from a distance

From a distance
You look like my friend
Even though we are at war
From a distance, I can't comprehend
What all this war is for

From a distance, there is harmony
And it echoes through the land

It's the hope of hopes
It's the love of loves
It's the heart of every man

It's the hope of hopes
It's the love of loves
It's the song of every man

From a distance
The world looks blue and green
And the snow-capped mountains white
From a distance
The ocean meets the stream
And the eagle takes to flight

From a distance, there is harmony
And it echoes through the land
It's the voice of hope
It's the voice of peace
It's the voice of every man

From a distance
We all have enough
And no one is in need
There are no guns, no bombs, no diseases
No hungry mouths to feed

From a distance, we are instruments
Marching in a common band
Playing songs of hope
Playing songs of peace
They're the songs of every man

God is watching us, God is watching us
God is watching us from a distance

From a distance
You look like my friend
Even though we are at war
From a distance, I can't comprehend
What all this war is for

From a distance, there is harmony
And it echoes through the land
It's the hope of hopes
It's the love of loves
It's the heart of every man

It's the hope of hopes
It's the love of loves
It's the song of every man

JULIE GOLD's song "From a Distance" was sent to me in the spring of 1986 by our mutual friend and fellow songwriter, Christine Lavin. I listened to the tape of Julie's solo voice and piano nonstop for days until I finally called Julie to express to her myself just how important I thought the message in her song was.

We had the opportunity to actually meet in person during my next visit to New York. I had just signed with MCA Records out of Nashville at that time, with Tony Brown co-producing my work, and we were just beginning the preproduction work on my first album for that label, Lone Star State of Mind. Tony Brown had fallen in love with Julie's song by that time and hoped I would record it. With Julie's belief in my voice to carry her song and the depth of her love for humanity that song shares with us all, Tony Brown and I recorded it the first week of July that summer of 1986. It was one of those very rare times in recording where everyone involved felt they had been part of something extremely profound and important.

I know that when Tony Brown and I left the studio that summer evening we both looked up at the twilight sky above us and the earth around us with a very different view than we'd had early that morning before recording Julie Gold's incredible piece of work. We were both proud and, indeed, humbled to have been a part of bringing that song to hearts, minds, and ears worldwide. We shared a great hope that this song would one day be sung by many voices for all of our children and by our children on again to the next of us.

Since that summer day of 1986 to the present, I have had the honor of recording and performing "From a Distance" in four languages—English, Spanish, German, and French. I've seen it grow from a dream to a reality in being a global anthem. I have heard it played as a wake-up call for astronauts on the space shuttle, and heard it sung by some of the greatest voices of our time, including Bette Midler. I have been overwhelmed by having the joy of singing it with the pristine and unique voices of Donna Summer and Raul Malo for the Atlantic Olympics Record, with the three of us combining all four languages.

I have been elated to have performed the song with my own band, the Blue Moon Orchestra, around the world, as well as being invited to sing it with several symphony companies, including the Nashville Symphony and the Boston Pops. Throughout the years, performing Julie's song on television appearances; in my live performance film, *One Fair Summer Evening*; with my band leader, pianist James Hooker; to multiple performances on the world's most prestigious stages—including the Royal Albert Hall in London and Carnegie Hall in New York—no performance has ever been as dear as performing it once, with Julie on piano, at Carnegie in the fall of 1987. That performance reminded me, yet again, of just how moved I was that spring day in 1986 when I played that tape and heard this song in Julie's own voice for the first time. The song has become, with each voice singing her message of beauty and grace, a rare and true classic and a great love with lasting hope for humanity.

It remains a brilliant treasure in world music, and Julie Gold remains one of the most selfless and uniquely gifted songwriters of our time. Both Julie and her songs are sparkling jewels in that crown designated for the art of writing.

Des de lejos (from a distance),
NANCI GRIFFITH
Franklin, Tennessee
Winter, 1997